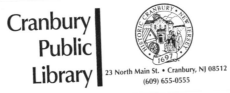

Friendship

A Level Three Reader

By Cynthia Klingel and Robert B. Noyed

The **Child's World**®

On the cover...
These friends are laughing as they go to school.

Published by The Child's World®, Inc.

PO Box 326
Chanhassen, MN 55317-0326
800-599-READ
www.childsworld.com

Special thanks to the Dunsing, Giroux, Melaniphy, Rodriguez, and Toral families, and to the staff and students of Alessandro Volta School for their help and cooperation in preparing this book.

Photo Credits
© Bettmann/CORBIS: 25
© CORBIS: 22
© 1997 Ken Chernus/FPG International: cover
© Michael Newman/PhotoEdit: 10
© Myrleen Cate/PhotoEdit: 14
© Myrleen Ferguson/PhotoEdit: 26
© Romie Flanagan: 6, 13, 18, 21
© Stephen Simpson/FPG International: 3, 5
© Tom McCarthy/Unicorn Stock Photos: 17
© Yellow Dog Productions/Image Bank: 9

Project Coordination: Editorial Directions, Inc.
Photo Research: Alice K. Flanagan

Library of Congress Cataloging-in-Publication Data
Klingel, Cynthia Fitterer.
Friendship / by Cynthia Klingel and Robert B. Noyed.
     p. cm. — (Wonder books-an early reader)
Includes index.
Summary: Provides everyday examples of what it means to be a friend.
ISBN 1-56766-088-6 (alk. paper)
1. Friendship—Juvenile literature. [1. Friendship.]
I. Noyed, Robert B. II. Title. III. Wonder books/an early reader (Chanhassen, Minn.)
BJ1533.F8 K55 2002
177'.62—dc21
                         2001007952

What is **friendship**? Friendship is showing that you like and care about other people. There are many ways to show friendship.

There are two parts to friendship. One part is being a good friend. The other part is having a good friend. They go together. A special friendship is a wonderful thing.

At school, you see a girl sitting by herself at lunch. You were going to sit with some friends at another table. Friendship is going to sit with that person so she will not be alone.

People of different ages can be friends, too. You might be a good friend to a neighbor who is older than you. When it snows, maybe he will teach you how to shovel the sidewalk.

Your friend falls and hurts her knee. You help get her home. You stay with her until she feels better. Friendship is being with your friends when they are hurt.

If you are sad, it helps to have a good friend. You can tell your friend why you are sad. Your friend will listen and help you feel better. Being a good friend means being a good listener.

Friendship is also important when you are happy. You can tell your friend when something good happens to you. Sharing happiness is part of friendship.

Friendship is about other kinds of sharing, too. Sometimes friends share a tasty snack. Sometimes they share their time together. Friends also share a laugh. And friends share a hug!

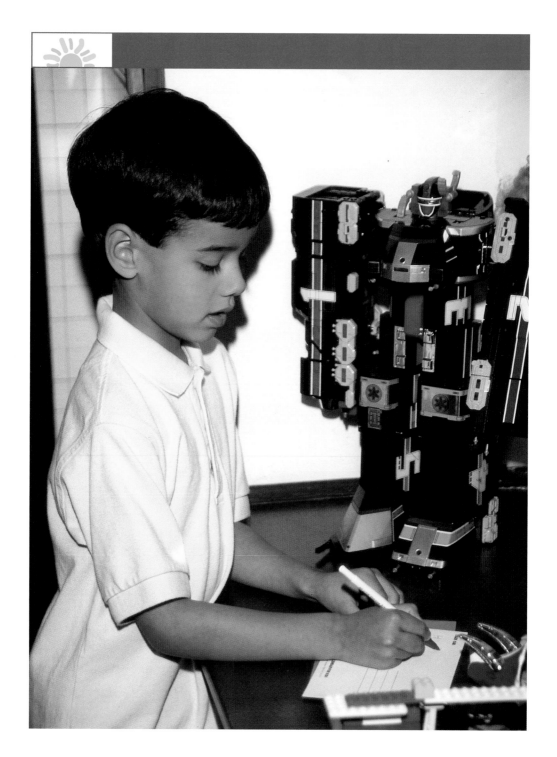

Sometimes friends live in different cities or even different countries. They share friendship by talking on the phone or sending letters or e-mail. People can have friends all over the world.

Friendship means remembering your friends at special times. When your friend has a birthday, you can give him a gift or card. Remembering a friend's special day shows you care.

Many people in history have shown friendship. One of these people was Anne Sullivan. She was a teacher for Helen Keller, who could not hear, see, or talk. Anne Sullivan was also Helen's best friend. In fact, Anne Sullivan stayed with Helen even when Helen no longer needed a teacher.

This picture shows Anne Sullivan reading to Helen Keller.

23

Anne Sullivan showed her friendship for Helen Keller in many ways. Anne **encouraged** Helen when Helen was a child. Later, Anne lived with Helen and helped her with everyday **tasks**. When Helen Keller became a famous speaker, Anne helped her travel around the country. Anne was a wonderful friend.

This is a picture of Anne Sullivan (right) and Helen Keller on a trip. →

Friendship is important. Being a friend makes you feel good. It also makes others happy. We can never have too many friends. How have you shown friendship today?

At Home

- Talk to your brothers or sisters if they are feeling sad.

- Ask your parents if you can help them with anything around the house.

- Plan a family game night.

At School

- Help a classmate with his or her homework.

- Invite a new classmate to play with you and your friends at recess.

- Bring a special snack to share with your classmates on your birthday.

In Your Community

- Give your outgrown clothes or toys to a younger neighbor.

- Invite a neighbor who lives alone to share a meal with your family.

- Introduce a new neighbor to other people in your neighborhood.

Glossary

encouraged (en-KUR-ijd)
To encourage people is to support them and help them feel good about what they are doing.

friendship (FREND-ship)
A friendship is when people care about each other and know each other well.

tasks (TASKS)
A task is a job or duty.

Index

To Find Out More

Books

Cannon, Janell. *Stellaluna.* New York: Harcourt Brace, 1993.

Kidd, Ronald. *Building Friends.* Atlanta, Ga.: Habitat for Humanity International, 1996.

Klingel, Cynthia, and Robert B. Noyed. *Helen Keller.* Chanhassen, Minn.: Child's World, 2002.

Lobel, Arnold. *Frog and Toad Are Friends.* New York: HarperCollins Children's Books, 1979.

Lundell, Margo. *A Girl Named Helen Keller.* New York: Scholastic, 1995.

Web Sites

Facts about Friends
http://kidshealth.org/kid/feeling/friend/about_friends.html
For more information about friendship.

Meet Cool People
www.hud.gov/kids/people.html
To find out how you can help others in your community.

Note to Parents and Educators

Welcome to Wonder Books®! These books provide text at three different levels for beginning readers to practice and strengthen their reading skills. Additionally, the use of nonfiction text provides readers the valuable opportunity to *read to learn*, not just to learn to read.

These leveled readers allow children to choose books at their level of reading confidence and performance. Nonfiction Level One books offer beginning readers simple language, word choice, and sentence structure as well as a word list. Nonfiction Level Two books feature slightly more difficult vocabulary, longer sentences, and longer total text. In the back of each Nonfiction Level Two book are an index and a list of books and Web sites for finding out more information. Nonfiction Level Three books continue to extend word choice and length of text. In the back of each Nonfiction Level Three book are a glossary, an index, and a list of books and Web sites for further research.

State and national standards in reading and language arts emphasize using nonfiction at all levels of reading development. Wonder Books® fill the historical void in nonfiction material for primary grade readers with the additional benefit of a leveled text.

About the Authors

Cynthia Klingel has worked as a high school English teacher and an elementary school teacher. She is currently the curriculum director for a Minnesota school district. Cynthia lives with her family in Mankato, Minnesota.

Robert B. Noyed started his career as a newspaper reporter. Since then, he has worked in school communications and public relations at the state and national level. Robert lives with his family in Brooklyn Center, Minnesota.